Red Drops on White Snow

By Cypher Lx

Chapter One

Queen Fiona

Once upon a time, in the war-torn Middle Kingdom, there stood a majestic castle. King Owen was a kind ruler, fair to his people and generous to a fault. His kingdom was envied by several surrounding territories for the bounty and good fortune his people enjoyed. Two such kingdoms waged war upon him to take it for their own. The turmoil was in its eleventh year, and had grown in intensity, when King Owen took a young and beautiful wife, born of an equally fortunate kingdom from the East, as his queen. He had rejected the notion of an arranged marriage to the daughter of an enemy for the sake of a tenuous peace treaty. His wedding to Fiona was the result of years of courtship from the time their fathers had introduced them in their childhood. They cherished one another, which made it all the more painful when Owen joined his armies on the battlefield. Now, in the darkness of the winter months, he would journey out again to ensure his men were fed and clothed properly during the storms. This departure was more difficult on them than in previous times, for Fiona was in her eighth month with their first child and suffered a cough.

"I will send someone else in my stead," King Owen said as he held her in his arms. "You and our child need me here."

"If you do not see to them, they will begin to lose hope," she responded, her voice lilting with hints of her Eastern heritage. It was one of her many attributes that endeared her to him. "The men need to know that you will always stand with them and that their Queen will not interfere with your duties. It is not as if you are journeying farther than the border. You will return in but a few weeks time to see the birth of our child. There are many in our household who would see to our safety in your absence."

Gently, he twisted strands of her silken hair around his fingers as he gazed into her eyes.

"You speak wisely, my love. I shall make haste in my travels so that I may return in time.

Promise me that you will heed the physician's treatments so that you are in good health."

"I will. I promise."

King Owen kissed her, savoring her scent and touch. Her fair hair smelled of rosemary and cedar, and her complexion was like the purest cream. He then knelt down in front of her, speaking to their unborn child.

"Take care of your mother and be strong."

Standing once again, he embraced Fiona longingly before departing through the large oak doors into the snowy courtyard where his steed awaited, alongside carts of supplies to be taken to the battle.

Fiona insisted on the doors being left open until she saw him pass through the gates. Immediately, she felt the emptiness he left behind. The phantom sensation of his chainmail against her bosom faded as she began to shiver from the winter wind. Her lady-in-waiting rushed up behind her, wrapping a fur cloak around her shoulders.

"If you allow your cough to get worse as you see him off, you will not do him or that child of yours any good," she spoke as she fastened a clasp in the front to secure it. "You can watch from the southern spire. Every day, if that is your wish. I will have a fire prepared to keep the dampness away."

And so it was that each and every day the Queen seated herself by the window to work her embroidery by the light of day, or by candlelight if she could not sleep. Despite the castle physician's best efforts, Fiona's health continued to decline. Her cough worsened and even the strongest mixture of horehound and diapenidion only gave her the smallest relief. She took her meals in the tower and slept in the bed that had been moved there so there would be less strain to her fragile constitution. Still, Fiona watched from the window for the first sign of her husband's return, a raven perched on a nearby parapet her only company when she was left alone. She could see fires burning in the distance. Were they the signs of war or merely large fires for the encampments, she could not tell. The dark smoke billowed into the cold air, mixing with the low, grey clouds that hung in the sky.

A little more than two weeks had passed. Fiona had suffered a particularly nasty coughing fit which left her feeling overheated. She opened the window to let the winter air in. Snowflakes fell like soft feathers onto the ebony wood window frame. The color of the wood reminded her of the King whose hair was just as dark, unlike the pale gold of her own. Sitting with her embroidery once again, a shudder went through her body as the breeze brushed against the sweat that glistened on her skin, causing her to prick her finger with the needle. Three drops of blood fell upon the window frame that now had a layer of snow. She marveled at the brilliance of the red against the white background, thinking it to be the most beautiful thing she had ever seen. As the light began to fade from the sky, her thoughts turned to that of her unborn child.

"I wish for my child to be as beautiful as this. To have hair the color of the darkest ebony wood, the complexion of virgin snow, and lips the color of blood," she spoke aloud.

The raven that had kept vigil with her took flight and landed on the window frame, and seemed to glance down at the frozen droplets of Fiona's blood in the snow, pecking at one of the red beads and seeming to swallow it. She was somewhat startled that the bird would come so close.

"Is that all you would wish?"

Surely it was her illness that made her hear things and she looked around the room to be certain that no one else was in her presence.

"Is that all you would wish," the voice asked again.

"You can speak!" Fiona exclaimed.

"I can do many things," the raven said. "Would you invite me in? For I have something to offer."

"What is your name, raven?"

"I am called William, Queen Fiona. Would you invite me in?"

Fiona hesitated a moment. Was this an hallucination caused by the medicines she had been given? In her childhood, she had heard that ravens could be trained to speak and were very intelligent creatures, but never in her life had she known of one that could speak its own mind without prompting.

"I would invite you in," she finally responded, "only if you intend no harm."

"That is something I would never wish on anyone of King Owen's house," said the raven as it crossed the threshold of the window frame and into the tower room.

The raven hopped across the floor toward the fireplace and shook its feathers free of snow as it began to transform into something much larger and resembling a man, with hair as dark as the raven and skin like flawless alabaster, clad in black armor and cloak. Fiona stared in disbelief and feared she might die of fright, her heart pounding in her chest and her breathing becoming even more labored than it already had been. A cough wracked her lungs again. The man figure poured a goblet of water and assisted her to take sips, calming the

spasms in her throat. Fiona began to feel more at

ease and the man took a knee before her. He was

young. Perhaps in his twentieth year if she were to

guess. And he was quite handsome, almost

unnaturally so. There were rumors of people who

were ethereal in their beauty, but feared and nearly

driven to extinction through genocidal acts of other

kingdoms.

"King Owen has been kind to our Kingdom,

as was his father before him, and his father's father

before that. The people of the North are outcasts to

the West and South kingdoms. They fear us

because of what we are. However, the lineage of

your King has always come to our aid in times of

war and we have been returning the favor in kind

these past eleven years. This Kingdom has always

been the exception, which is just one of the many reasons why the other kingdoms hope for his downfall. As his most loyal knight, my King has sent me with an offer. It is not without cost, unfortunately. There is only so much we can give. There are some things that are beyond even our abilities. Please, Queen Fiona, tell me, is the beautiful appearance of your child the only thing that you wish?"

Given this new information and some time to accept what had just been presented to her, Fiona thought for a moment.

"Of course, any mother would wish for her child to be very fair in appearance," she began, "but I would also wish for this child to be forever in good health and a worthy heir to carry on the legacy that has been told to me this night."

"Very well," the man replied. "Though I can have no influence on how your child may look, I am certain that she will have the beauty of her mother and the wisdom of her father. And now I must offer you a choice. It is yours alone to make."

A single tear fell down Fiona's cheek. "So, I am to have a daughter?"

"Does this displease you?"

"No, not at all. I would just wish for one more thing, whether it is within your power or not. I would wish that she finds the same love that her father and I share, and not be forced to marry into a house that will treat her as a spoil of war," she said.

"That is not something I can guarantee," the knight said with a slight frown. "However, I can watch over her and be her guide when I am able. Of course, you must make your choice first. This is what I offer. My dear Queen Fiona, you are very ill. More than your physician knows. It is not his fault. There is nothing that he would be able to do for you even if he had the knowledge of your malady. I can save one of you, but not both. To save your life means certain death for your daughter. To save your daughter and ensure her long life, you will most certainly die soon after her birth. It is difficult to explain. The process to save your life at this very moment would kill the child in your womb. To attempt the process after her birth would turn you into something like an abomination. Not much more than a walking corpse. The child's health is also in danger, but a smaller portion of the elixir given to her immediately after she enters the world will restore her quickly. Your last choice is to do nothing at all. Your will is mine to obey."

With this new knowledge, Fiona did not hesitate.

"I would give my life if it means my child will live well and happy."

"Even if it means leaving King Owen to mourn the death of his beloved wife? You must be sure in your decision, for the time of birth is quickly approaching and I will be unable to return should you change your mind. The battle to the West is escalating and I must lead my own garrison to prevent the enemy from gaining ground," William said, wondering if the Queen was truly as selfless as she claimed to be in this moment.

"He will understand that I have done this out of love. He will look into her eyes each day and see me gazing back at him. He will know that I have done this for him and for our daughter, that she may give him many years of joy knowing that she is the best of both of us. I will regret nothing as long as I know she will survive."

"So be it," he said, reaching into his cloak and pulling out a small glass vial containing dark liquid. After removing the cork, William gently took her hand and brought the finger she had pricked to his lips. She felt a slight sting, and he placed her finger, flowing with fresh blood, above the opening of the vial, capturing the drops as they fell. "Your blood will make it easier for the infant to stomach," he explained, recorking the vial. He closed his eyes as if in thought. "King Owen requested that a midwife from my homeland be sent to you. It seems she has arrived. I will leave this in her care. She knows what is to be done."

In less than a moment, the black clad knight transformed into a raven once again, hopping up onto the window frame and spreading his wings to take flight.

"Sir William?"

The large bird turned his head to look at Fiona.

"Thank you," she said, and the raven bowed his head before taking off into the night.

Each day after, Fiona thought of William's offer and knew that she had made the right decision. However, she grew concerned as another week passed by and her daughter moved less and less inside of her. This took a toll on her own health. Her appetite left her and her coughing fits worsened. She needed assistance to take the few short steps from her bed to the chair by the window, where she continued to watch for any sign of her husband's return. The midwife had arrived the very night Sir William had appeared to her. The woman was much older, but still held the same ethereal presence. The other staff of the castle gave the woman a wide berth when she entered the room, and Fiona would hear them speaking in hushed tones when she would leave. They would say things like "night creatures" or "monsters" or "children of the devil", but the midwife either did not hear these insults, or chose to ignore them, and showed the utmost kindness to Fiona.

The evening came that Fiona felt the first pains of labor. She thought she could see the caravan returning to the castle gates from the window. The excitement was too much for her frail body, causing a cascade of physical events. Her screams could be heard echoing through the stone halls, only interrupted by the rough coughing spells that could no longer be controlled by elixirs or water. Fiona's body was hemorrhaging badly. Nothing the physician had done could prevent it. The infant was in the wrong position and the midwife reached deep inside Fiona to turn the child, the unbearable pain causing Fiona to lose consciousness. The only thing to be done was to remove the child without the aid of her mother. The midwife knew the damage would be irreparable, but she had been given instruction to save the infant at all costs, despite the resounding objections of the physician and lady-in-waiting. And so it was that the Princess was born. The woman carried her away quickly, wiping her face clean and deftly uncorking the vial she was given with one hand, placing it to the baby's lips, hoping the elixir would do its work and make the child draw breath before her heart ceased beating. She listened closely as the beats grew stronger, and the child gasped and let out a hearty cry. King Owen burst into the room as the midwife finished cleaning the blood from his daughter, and Fiona's lady-in-waiting covered her Queen's exposed and torn body from his view, leaving her to look as if she was merely enjoying a rest from what had just transpired. Fiona stirred slightly hearing her child's cries and Owen approached her bedside, sitting next to her and holding her in his arms, smoothing the hair from her forehead. Slowly she opened her eyes.

"You have returned," she spoke quietly as she looked up at him, her voice hoarse.

"Yes, my love. Sir William sent a messenger to the front to deliver news of your condition," he said. His throat tightened with each word. "His letter told me of your agreement."

"Please do not think ill of me. Hold my memory close to your heart. Love our daughter enough for the both of us. Promise me."

Tears formed in the King's eyes. "I could never think ill of you, and I will cherish her until the end of my days," he said, kissing her lightly on the forehead.

The midwife placed the child delicately into Fiona's arms. Her daughter was indeed beautiful. Ebony hair clung damply to the infant's head. Her cupid bow lips were the color of blood. And her skin…

"Snow white," Fiona whispered on her last breath.

Chapter Two

Queen Maurelle

A year had passed by, and King Owen overcame his grief gradually by enjoying every moment he could spare with his little Princess. He knew the time had come that he should take a new wife. However, as much as the thought displeased him, he also knew that it would be a marriage of practicality. He could never love anyone as deeply as he did Fiona, but his daughter needed a mother, and his Kingdom needed a queen. After much consideration and negotiation with the ruler of one of the two Southern kingdoms that continued to wage war on his people, he took Lady Maurelle as his wife. She was quite the beauty, but she did not hold his heart. Only Snow White and the memory of Fiona had that privilege.

Queen Maurelle was a proud woman and her vanity surpassed that of anyone. She immediately dismissed the midwife from the North, despite her excellence in the raising of Snow White. Though the woman was older than Maurelle, she could not bear to be compared to someone who had such a presence about her. Even the staff who had initially rebuked the woman welcomed her into the house when they saw how well she cared for the Princess. The King reluctantly agreed, if only to keep the peace with his new wife. With her arrival came a list of demands, including a special room for her looking-glass, which no one was permitted to enter. On her first day in the castle, Maurelle locked herself in the room with her prized possession.

"Looking-glass, Looking-glass, on the wall, who in this land is the fairest of all?"

The mirrored surface rippled, her reflection distorting slightly before returning to its flattering image. Then a voice answered from within its depths.

"You, my Queen, art the fairest of all."

This pleased her, satisfied that no others in this new kingdom could compare with her beauty, for the looking-glass could not lie. The magicks imbued within the golden frame would not allow it. And so, she began devising her plan to solidify her role as queen. She knew that she would need to bear the King a son to nullify Snow White's claim as heir to the throne. Though the child was little more than an infant, a day would come when the

Princess would rule over the Queen should Owen precede them both in death. Dabbling in the dark arts brought her to this place, though she had not known that the former Queen was with child when she had placed the curse upon her. Somehow, Snow White had survived the spell that had been cast.

It was several months until Queen Maurelle could lure the King to her bed. His love for Fiona was still strong, even two years after her death. It was finally after she discovered the proper combination of henbane, belladonna, mandrake, and datura that she slipped the concoction into his ale at supper. While it had the desired effect, she was angered when he called out Fiona's name, such was the hallucinatory effect that made him believe his love was sharing the most intimate of moments with him once again. Had she known of her success, she would have stabbed him in the heart right then.

The Queen's joy was short-lived. The magicks she used in conjunction with the potion specifically entailed that only a male child would be born to her. After the third month she miscarried. The product of her trickery had failed her. No. The King had failed her. It was his duty as much as hers to produce a male heir, and now he refused to even share meals with her for fear that she would drug him again. While the King could have had her punished, or even put to death, she knew it was the treaty that prevented him from doing so. Had she foreseen the obstacles which continued to vex her, she would have insisted a provision be made within the treaty to guarantee that the Princess would never come to rule. Maurelle was still given all the luxuries that she wished, except for what she wanted most. A son to take the throne. Her anger increased further each time she had to bear witness to King Owen's interactions with Snow White, which became more frequent as the girl learned to speak.

"Father? How was I named," the Princess asked.

King Owen pulled the child up onto his knee and looked into her brilliant blue eyes, taking a deep breath before telling her the story.

"Your mother, rest her soul, wanted a child that would combine the best of qualities. And so, you were born, with hair as dark as my own and as soft as hers. You have her kind heart and eyes and my love for everything that was a part of her. On the night you came into the world, snow fell from the sky, pure and untouched and whiter than parchment. Your mother's last words were 'snow white' as she gazed upon your sleeping face. We had not yet chosen a moniker for you and this is how you came to have your name, Snow White, my dear child. It is to honor your mother and the only memory of her that you may always carry with you. May you always bring happiness to those you encounter such as she did in her life," he said, gently kissing the top of her head.

The girl giggled and kissed her father on the cheek before jumping down and playing with her dolls that had been momentarily forgotten at his feet.

Such was the scene nearly every day, and it sickened Maurelle. Her jealousy seethed within her that she could not garner similar attentions from the

King, her husband. And then there were the gifts

that came for the child. Some would send toys,

others sent finely tailored clothing as she grew.

And each year, on the girl's birthday, a knight from

the North, clad head to toe in black armor, would

personally deliver a single, perfectly red apple to

Snow White, quietly watching from behind the

visor of his helmet as she enjoyed every bite. From

the highest nobility to the lowest servant, everyone

loved the girl. They would marvel at her humility,

her kindness to all, human and animal alike, and her

beauty. The Queen found herself in her private

room more and more often.

"Looking-glass, Looking-glass, on the wall,

who in this land is the fairest of all?"

Each time, the glass would ripple before returning to its flawless reflection of the Queen before speaking.

"You, my Queen, art the fairest of all."

Though the looking-glass was unable to tell anything but the truth, Maurelle thought she could hear doubt in the thing's voice. Still, she remained satisfied that she was more beautiful than any other.

By the Princess' seventh year, the Queen had still not gained favor with the King. He did not treat her poorly, and still ensured that she lived in comfort, however, she was merely greeted cordially while Snow White garnered the attention of her father and the entire household. Her ebony locks shone in the sun as she played in the courtyard. Her pale skin accented her blood red lips, which became fuller as she grew. The child was indeed beautiful. And Maurelle hated her for it.

Again, she asked her magickal possession, "Looking-glass, Looking-glass, on the wall, who in this land is the fairest of all?"

Her image rippled and warped before steadying. Her face looked duller and the voice within hesitated.

"My Queen, thou art fairer than all who are here, but more beautiful still is Snow White, year by year."

Fury grew in Queen Maurelle's cold heart. The child who should have died with her mother was now surpassing her in beauty. It was intolerable. She paced the room. The King would not give her a son, and Snow White was treated as a beloved treasure. Even the looking-glass favored the girl. After an hour had passed, the Queen devised a new plan. One that would rid her of Snow White and guarantee her the throne when the King died.

In her chambers, she sat at her desk, pulling out a quill and parchment. She began writing with renewed purpose, almost frenzied in her scribblings.

"Garrick, as the most trusted in my service, I require your skills as a huntsman. This task is of the utmost importance and secrecy. I trust that you will be as loyal as the gold I will provide when you have proven the deed is done. I wish for you to take the child, Snow White, into the woods and slit her throat. You will bring to me her lungs and liver as tokens of the kill. What you do with her remains is of no concern to me. Make a belt with her hair, if you wish. For that may be the only thing of value."

Then she scrolled the parchment and tied it to the leg of her personal falcon, which followed her every command. It took flight, and she smiled for the first time in years.

Chapter Three

Garrick, The Huntsman

A falcon landed on a branch near the place where Garrick felled a deer. He immediately recognized the bird and approached cautiously to remove the scroll it carried. Once he read the letter, he knew immediately that he would obey. Garrick loved the Queen, though she would never return his affections. It was her beauty that had bewitched him. He had left the only home he had known to follow her to this new land. It was her cold heart that had turned his own to stone. Killing for her became his only pleasure, whether it be for her exotic requests for nightly supper, as some creatures were rare and difficult to find, or her desire to rid the world of anyone who defied her.

He loaded the deer onto his cart and covered it with heavy oilcloth to keep the scavenger birds from pecking at its flesh as he took it to the castle. It was nightfall as he arrived. Stowing the cart in the shadows, he removed the carcass to the kitchen for it to be butchered. Then he waited until the wee hours, when most of the staff and household were sound asleep. Garrick slipped silently into Snow White's bedchambers. The Princess slumbered deeply and was easy enough to carry away without so much as a sound or a stir. Into the dark night, he crept with the sleeping child, and laid her in the cart, covering her with the tarpaulin so she would not be seen by any watchful eyes as he passed through the gate. Deeper and deeper he pulled the cart into the woods, for if the child let out a scream, no one within the castle walls would hear.

The first rays of dawn filtered through the trees when he found a clearing and stopped. Unsheathing his dagger, Garrick pulled the cloth away, revealing the girl. As the morning light struck her face, she opened her bleary eyes as he raised the blade to pierce her innocent heart. Snow White scurried to the corner of the cart, eyes wide with fear and filling with tears.

"Please leave me my life," she cried. "What evil have I done to be punished this way?"

Garrick, struck by the child's countenance, lowered his blade. "My Queen commands that this deed must be done. I know not of your crime, other than you have no favor with her. And my duty is to obey her will."

Snow White's tears flowed freely. "I have committed no crime other than to be my father's daughter. Please, if she wishes for me to never return, I will run away into the forest. She will never have to gaze upon me again. Please, dear huntsman, spare my life."

The child was beautiful. That much Garrick could see now that she was no longer shrouded in darkness. He tended not to speak nor look upon the residents of the castle, preferring not to have conversation. Had he seen this child before, he wondered if his unquestioning loyalty would have wavered. Perhaps that was her only crime, for he knew the Queen's vanity exceeded that of any other. And he took pity on the child then. A beauty such as Snow White's was rare. To have beauty and a kind heart was rarer still. She possessed both.

"Run away, then, child," he said, placing the dagger back in its sheath. "Run away and never return. The wild animals of the forest will surely make you their meal before the day's end, but I shall have a clear conscience that it was not I who took your life."

"Thank you, dear huntsman," she said, her voice still trembling. She climbed from the cart and ran until he could see her no more.

Though, now Garrick had no proof of the girl's demise and would be punished severely for his disobedience. He allowed the child's beauty to soften his heart. As if by some magic, a young bear came into the clearing, unafraid of the huntsman.

"I am grateful for your sacrifice," he whispered to the creature before gingerly slitting its throat and cutting out its lungs and liver.

Garrick made the journey back to the castle with his tokens placed in a resin lined box. Before Maurelle he knelt, in the privacy of her chambers, and opened the box for her to peer inside.

"For you, my Queen."

"Wonderful! Wonderful!" she exclaimed. "Have them prepared for my supper and I shall pay you your reward."

"As you wish, my Queen."

He took the organs to the kitchen and watched as the cook prepared them. The lungs were drained and salted and coated in flour as onions browned in a pan. The seasoned lungs were added to the pan and cooked. Finally, a blend of tomatoes, parsley, garlic, and a generous portion of white wine were added to the mixture. The liver was lightly seasoned with salt and pepper and cooked in another pan with onions. Once the plates were finished and dressed, Garrick took it upon himself to deliver the meal and stood by silently as the Queen devoured every last morsel.

"How delectable," she said after taking a sip of wine. "So tender was the lung. Such perfect seasoning. And the liver was delightful. I regret that I did not also request her heart. Surely, it would have been as pure as the rest." She pushed a small satchel across the table.

Though Garrick knew the truth of the wicked Queen's supper, he also knew that, should he hesitate, she would suspect that trickery had been involved. So, he stowed the purse away and bowed deeply.

"Always your loyal servant, my Queen."

Chapter Four

Snow White

The young girl ran and ran as fast as her legs could carry her. She had gone deep into the forest and could no longer see the castle spires behind her. Snow White's tears continued to flow. Why did her stepmother hate her so much to order her death? Had she done something to offend her? Had she broken something dear to her? She could think of nothing. Every day she would speak to the Queen cordially, as was taught to her when speaking to her elders and other members of the royal household. Her father had even instructed her to treat those who served them with the utmost kindness. The King reminded her daily that to treat others with respect and kindness will garner the same in return, and that she must always heed this advice when she was of age to take the throne. The tears flowed freely again as she now knew that she would never again see her beloved father. And what must her stepmother have said for him to agree to such a severe punishment? Certainly, he still loved her and must be suffering as much sorrow as she.

Her pace slowed as she grew more and more exhausted. The words of the huntsman echoed in her head, keeping her feet moving, even as her eyelids began to close. And yet, no beasts had come near. They passed her by without much more than a look in her direction. Still, Snow White was frightened. She had never ventured beyond the castle walls and wondered if the huntsman would regret his decision to let her flee. So, she kept going as long as her legs could carry her, and even then, until the evening when she could no longer see more than a small distance in front of her. It was then that she collapsed on a soft bed of moss, tired and so very hungry. As the sun made its final descent, Snow White, still in her nightclothes, shivered from the chill, then trembled in renewed fear as she heard a rustling in the brush. She listened and watched the darkness closely, and as the moon slowly rose above the treetops, she could swear she saw a shadow coming nearer. So, this was to be her end, just as the huntsman had spoken. She closed her eyes and waited for the beast to attack. It stalked toward her, its feet grazing fallen leaves and twigs, until she could feel the creature's warm breath upon her face. After a long moment that seemed an eternity, she opened her eyes and was face to face with a large wolf with fur as dark as the night. However, instead of terror, she suddenly felt comfort. The beast bowed its head and pushed an apple to her with its muzzle. Cautiously, she reached for the nourishment the animal offered, and picked it up.

"Thank you, dear friend," she whispered.

The wolf flanked her and then lay down, watching as she took each bite. When she had finished, her eyes grew heavy, and she once again rested herself on the moss. The beast moved next to her, and she could feel the softness of its fur, the thickness of it warm against her cold skin, and she curled up into the wolf's side and fell into a deep slumber. As she slept, she dreamed of a comely young man dressed in dark colored finery suited for royalty.

"My dear, Snow White," he spoke in a kindly voice. "Such a tragedy this is. Your pure heart should not have to endure the wilds. Follow the path of the sun for two day's time. The wolf will be your companion by night. On the midday of the third, you will find a cottage. The men who reside within are miners under my employ. They will protect you and teach you things you must learn to one day return to your household and understand the subjects you will reign over as the true Queen. Heed their words and you will be the worthy heir your mother wished for you to become. Be strong, young princess."

He placed a light kiss to her forehead, then faded from her mind's eye.

Snow White opened her eyes to the first light of morning and the chill that had not yet left with the night. The wolf was no longer in her presence. A sadness filled her again, but she fought against the tears and did as she had been told. Even if it was merely a dream, she had nowhere else to go. As the day passed, she came across a small stream and rested near it for a short while after taking deep draughts of cool water. Then she journeyed on until she could no longer see the sun's rays and found a soft place to lie down. As promised, the wolf came to her. This time, it held a waterskin gingerly between its sharp teeth. It set the gift before her and took the position it had the night before, allowing her to curl close into its warm, soft fur. Her sleep was dreamless, yet she still felt comforted knowing that she was not alone.

Once again, the wolf had left Snow White before the sun fully breached the horizon, and she took up the waterskin to continue through the forest. The day passed in loneliness and only her thoughts of the wolf returning in the evening and the cottage the day to follow kept her walking steadily northwest. She wondered about the miners that lived in such a place. Then she thought herself silly, for it was a dream that told her they existed. Yet, the wolf was her companion, just as the young man promised. As she pondered these things, she suddenly discerned that she had no name for him and decided to call him her "prince", though she had no way of knowing what station he held. And during the lonely hours, she thought of the kingdom where he might live. In her mind's eye, his castle was built of darker stone with flecks of crystal that captured the moonlight. The people within were as kind as the household she had always known and were all very handsome in appearance. Though her prince had told her she would one day return home, she mused that she might find the place she imagined if that were to never happen. Before long it was evening again, and the wolf returned to her side with the gift of food, a hunk of bread and wedge of cheese tied with a wide red ribbon. Snow White reached out and lightly touched the muzzle of the large creature.

"Thank you, my dear friend, for these gifts," she said. "I will miss your company come morning."

She ate and then drank some of the water that was still left from the day. Sated, she curled into the side of the wolf for warmth for the last night. When she woke, she wondered if she would ever see the black wolf again, for today at midday she would come to the end of her journey if her dream held true. She tied the ribbon into her hair, keeping the strands away from her eyes as the wind blew through the trees. As the sun peaked, she came into a large clearing. There, in its midst, stood a cottage of stone and wood. Snow White was grateful to have found the place as her feet were pained from the stones and her nightclothes and legs had suffered the thorns of thick underbrush.

Snow White approached and rapped on the door, but was greeted with silence. Entering, she found that not a soul was inside. The cottage was small. Surely not enough space for grown men, she thought. And it was incredibly clean with everything in its proper place. A table covered in pristine white cloth held seven place settings containing servings of bread and fruit and wine, waiting for the return of the inhabitants. Against the wall were seven beds, each covered in a counterpane as white as snow. Snow White was terribly hungry and tired. As thankful as she was for the small gifts of food she had been given, it was not nearly enough for a girl of her young age after traveling for so long. She took but a small bite from each plate and sip from each cup so that none of the men would go without when they returned. Then she tried each bed until she found one that could comfort her to sleep for a while, and when she did, she spoke a prayer her father taught her before falling asleep.

Chapter Five

The Miners

After the sun had gone down and the darkness was already thick, the owners of the cottage returned and lit candles from their small lanterns. When the cottage was fully lighted, the seven men saw that someone had been there as things looked just slightly out of place. It was then that one of them found Snow White asleep on his bed. The others joined at his side and gazed down at the little girl.

"Oh, heavens," exclaimed one of the men.

"Is this the girl," another asked.

"The one we were told would come," said a third.

"Indeed, she is quite a lovely child," spoke a fourth.

The other three voiced their agreement and decided to allow her to sleep through the night, for they knew what she had endured to come to this place. After the men had eaten their supper, they pushed the remaining six beds together as quietly as could be so that they would all have a place to sleep until morning. And when the first rays came through the windows, they arose and prepared enough food for eight. When the girl awoke, she looked startled to see them.

"What is your name, child," one of them asked kindly to put her at ease.

"I am called Snow White," she answered.

"How have you come to be here? Certainly you have a family."

While the men were told of the girl, they were not aware of why she had ventured so deep into the forest alone.

"My step-mother wished me dead," said Snow White. "Were it not for the mercy of her huntsman, I would not be here. But he allowed me to flee from the fate of his blade. A dream told me to come here."

When the girl rose from the bed, she stood at their height. Though she was still young, they were not of the same stature as normal men. They were chosen to work in the mines because they had never grown to a full height, but were strong and capable, and the ceilings of the mines were low, which would cause injury to taller men. Every person in the kingdom they called home had a place, and all were treated well. Even deep in the woods, their King ensured there was nothing they did not have to live comfortably, though these men did much of their own building and such by their own choosing.

"And were you told that we will show you skills," another of the men asked Snow White.

"Indeed, I was," she said with awe. But it was not explained how they knew such a thing.

"Today and tomorrow we shall show you tasks that need to be done while we work in the mines. Once we return to our duties, in the evenings, after the meal, we will instruct you in subjects you would have learned had you not been driven from your home. If you do these things you shall want for nothing. Do you agree?"

"Oh, yes, good sirs! With all my heart, yes," she exclaimed.

For two days the men stayed with her to show her the chores. One taught her how to wash the bedding and clothes. Another taught her simple knitting and sewing to make repairs. The third taught her to dust and sweep. Fire starting and tending was shown to her by the fourth. Preparing meals had been the task of the fifth man. The two that had yet to show her anything were to be her tutors in writing, the arts, and the politics of the known kingdoms. On the third day, it was time for them to return to the mines looking for veins of copper and gold. They had instantly taken a liking to the child and were concerned for her welfare while she remained alone during the day.

"Take care, child. There may be a time in the future that your step-mother learns you were not killed. Beware of strangers that may wander through. Be sure to let no one in, for if she discovers you while we are gone, we cannot protect you from her wrath."

Snow White promised them that she would do as she was told. Each day they issued a similar warning before they went to the mines. In the evenings she welcomed them home with a clean house and freshly made meal. She also understood her lessons well. The miners grew more and more fond of her and knew that she would make a fair and just ruler if she were given the opportunity. All the more reason to ensure her safety for the years to come.

Each week a peddler of one kind or another would pass through on the way to the market that stood past the forest's edge. On those days the miners rested from their hard work and purchased small items they could not supply themselves. They acquired dresses for Snow White as she grew and shoes for her feet. She became like a daughter to them. The first year had passed without misfortune. And this was their wish for however long Snow White was to stay.

Chapter Six

The Middle Kingdom

King Owen was stricken with grief when it was discovered that Snow White was missing from her bed, not to be found anywhere within the castle walls.

"Find her," he ordered his men. "Let no place go unsearched. Even the smallest cupboard or deepest well." And immediately, they set to work, for they all loved the girl dearly and shared in the King's despair.

Upon seeing the Queen, he questioned her.

"Where is Snow White? For she was gone from her bedchamber and has not been seen by the household," he said angrily.

"My dear, Owen. I have not seen the child," she replied, turning to leave his presence.

"You give me no reason to believe you speak the truth."

Turning back to face him, a half smile left her expression.

"And you give me no reason to care. I am your wife, and still, you dote on that child and refuse to give me your affections. Perhaps she has run away, as spirited as she is. No doubt, she has just gone to play one of her silly games and wishes for you to seek her out. After all, she craves all the attentions you give to her. You have spoiled her, and now she gives you grief for it. I would expect that she will be punished for such a thing. But, no, you will not. You will embrace her as if she had come back from the dead. And if she is truly gone, there is nothing to be done about it, but that you have another heir."

When he did not answer, she continued on her way, and did not lift a finger to join the search.

His men looked for Snow White in every part of the castle, and the surrounding woods within a distance from the walls, but could not find any sign of her fate. Days turned into weeks and weeks into months. The only physical evidence of his beloved Fiona was now gone from him, and he fell into a deep depression. He ceased taking meals and slowly succumbed to his sadness with the hope that he would soon join his child and loving wife in death.

On that final day, his kingdom mourned. All except Queen Maurelle. Though she wore the mask of the grieving wife, in the privacy of her chambers she celebrated, for this was what she had worked to achieve. The throne was now hers and she would rule the kingdom as she saw fit. Not with the soft hand of King Owen, but with the iron fist of a true ruler. Her joy led her to the private room of her prized possession.

Twirling in front of her own reflection she asked, "Looking-glass, looking-glass, on the wall, who in this land is the fairest of all?"

She did not notice the hesitation, so absorbed she was in her private celebration. When she stopped her dance, she saw that her image appeared even duller than before.

"My Queen, thou art the fairest of all I see, but over the hills, where in a cottage men dwell, Snow White is still alive and well. And none is so fair as she."

"He betrayed me!" she screamed. "Garrick betrayed me!"

Storming out of the room, the heavy door slamming hard behind her, she took the arm of the first guard she found in a fierce grip.

"Bring me the huntsman," she ordered.

The guard leapt into action, and she knew he feared her. This would be her first show of power. To show her kingdom that anyone who dared disobey her would be punished severely.

The huntsman arrived at her chambers flanked by guards. She dismissed them abruptly, leaving her alone with Garrick.

"Whose lungs and liver did I sup upon last year," she questioned.

"That of the child, Snow White, my Queen."

"Do not lie to me, Garrick! Did you believe that I would not discover the truth of your betrayal? You, my most loyal of servants. Now tell me, whose lungs and liver were prepared for me?"

She could see the fear shadow his eyes and her voice softened.

"Tell me, my dear Garrick and I will be kind to you."

"My Queen," he began with a tremble in his tone. "I could not do as you commanded. I stole her in the night and took her deep into the woods. My blade was poised to do the deed. But I could not murder a child so innocent of any crime other than that you did not favor her. I allowed her to run away, knowing that she would not survive the perils of the forest. I took the life of a bear cub in her stead. That is what you supped upon. Nothing more. But surely the child is dead."

"She lives still, Garrick. Were you so taken in by the wretched child's beauty?"

"I am at your mercy, my Queen. I shall seek her out and finish the task, if that is your wish."

Maurelle approached him, pressing her bosom against his chest and drawing a slender finger down his cheek. She watched his eyes close, knowing that this was the attention he so craved from her.

"No, Garrick. Your weakness will not be able to withstand her cunning a second time. I shall find another way."

She kissed him softly on the lips.

"You may leave me now," she said.

Garrick appeared both relieved and torn as he turned and opened the door. The guards had kept their post in the hallway.

"Take him to the cells," she ordered. "He is to be executed by beheading in the morning for all to see."

"Your mercy, my Queen," Garrick begged.

"For your betrayal, be grateful that I do not have you drawn and quartered," she responded coldly. "To lose your head is appropriate, as you have already accomplished that on your own. It is all the mercy I have to give."

With but a gesture, the guards took hold of Garrick's arms and pulled him away.

Alone once again, Queen Maurelle began pacing her chambers. She needed to be rid of Snow White. As long as the Princess lived, she could lay claim to the throne when she came of age. And the Queen knew that the people would readily accept her. Now, they would also know who had ordered her death. Everyone would believe the story she told. The girl's beauty sowed the jealousy in Maurelle's heart, but her audacity to live, despite efforts to the contrary, cultivated a deep hatred that would only die with Snow White's last breath.

The Queen spent the night walking the halls, rejecting one plan after another. In the morning, she took little joy in watching her huntsman's head fall into the awaiting basket as the crowd watched in horror. They had never witnessed such a thing before, and their expressions should have brought her happiness. On the contrary, the blood that sprayed from where Garrick's head was once attached reminded Maurelle of Snow White's red lips.

After days of contemplation, the Queen realized her folly in trusting another to carry out her wishes to kill Snow White. Though now, if the girl were to fall to a blade or some other violence,

Maurelle would immediately become suspect. The girl's demise must appear as an accident of some sort, then. The Queen knew of only one cottage in the forest as it was in a main thoroughfare for the peddlers to the market. She decided then what she must do and set about her plan.

With the power of her dark magicks, she disguised herself as an elderly peddler woman and made her way to where Snow White remained hidden from the world. When she came upon the cottage, the young girl was hanging freshly laundered bedclothes on twine strung between the trees for them to dry in the breeze. Snow White was indeed as beautiful as ever and the Queen had to quell the hatred in her heart to maintain her façade.

"Hello, my dear," the Queen spoke.

Snow White leapt in surprised. "Oh dear! You've given me a fright!"

"You have nothing to fear from me, child. I am but an elderly woman on her way to sell her wares in the market."

"Please do not think me rude," Snow White replied. "I did not expect to see a peddler passing through this day."

"Of course not, dear," the Queen laughed. "But I am old, and I travel slowly. Could I interest you in something special while I am here? Perhaps some new lacings for your bodice."

"Oh, I think not. For I am told not to speak to strangers and have already done so. I also have nothing to offer in payment."

"If it is payment that worries you so, then accept the lacings as a gift for taking the time from your chores to speak with an old woman. Choose any color you wish. They are made from the finest silks."

Snow White appeared to have no suspicion, which pleased the Queen, and she chose lacings that matched the red ribbon she wore in her hair.

"Excellent choice, my dear," the Queen said. "Please allow me to help you to replace the lacings you have. They look such a fright, so much wear they have seen."

The girl turned and the Queen removed the old lacings, threading the new with such quickness that could not be seen by Snow White. The Queen pulled the lacings tight. Much tighter than would allow one to breathe.

"Please," Snow White gasped. "I cannot…" And within moments the girl fell down as if dead.

Queen Maurelle cast off her illusion and looked down upon the motionless Snow White. "Now I am the most beautiful, you wicked child. You shall never find your place upon the throne."

Chapter Seven

The Return

The miners returned to the cottage later in the evening and knew something was amiss upon seeing the linens still on their lines. In the fading light, they found dear little Snow White lying on the ground. And though she appeared to be merely sleeping, she did not stir when they approached. They feared her dead and lifted her up to carry her into the cottage where they were able to see her more clearly. One of the men saw that she had new lacings that she had not possessed before and that they were laced too tightly. Quickly, he drew a blade and cut the silk, loosening the bodice. Snow White's breathe came lightly at first, but the men saw that she lived and were able to breathe more easily themselves, for they feared they had lost the child.

After a while, Snow White awoke fully and one of the miners gave her sips of wine.

"Tell us what happened to you, child," said one of the others. "Where did you get these lacings that nearly stole your breath?"

Snow White knew in her heart that she had done wrong in speaking with the elderly woman and hesitated to answer.

"Speak, child. You have nothing to fear from us. You shall not be punished."

"There was an old woman. A peddler, she said. I thought it odd, as others have only come through when you are not in the mines. She claimed to travel more slowly and gave me the lacings as a gift for being kind to her. But she made them tight, and I could not take in breath. That is the last I recall," she said as tears filled her eyes.

Each miner embraced her in turn to give her comfort.

"The Queen has found you out, it would seem," said one of the men. "It could be no other. For who else would wish harm upon our beautiful Snow White? But you must be more careful. She may now believe you to be truly dead. However, you must take no more chances. Speak to no one else unless we are here with you."

In the following weeks, the miners spent less time in the mines to ensure that Snow White was in good health and to watch for the Queen's return. It seemed that the girl was indeed believed to be dead, as they saw no signs of misdeeds from those who passed through. It was when the knight clad in black arrived that the men appeared both relieved and even more good mannered than Snow White had ever seen. This was the same knight that came to her each year when she still lived in the castle and, as before, he brought her an apple of the deepest red and watched silently from behind his visor as she consumed each bite. Never once had she heard the knight speak, not even to others. But still, he was given respect and so she knew that she could trust him.

In the evening, after her meal and lessons, Snow White fell into a deep sleep and dreamed of her prince once again. Together they walked a path at night through gardens with flowers she had never seen, and he taught her about each one.

"My dear, Snow White," he said, "you grow more beautiful by the year. Soon these flowers will pale in comparison. Continue to heed the warnings and lessons of the miners and you will surely become a worthy Queen as well."

With those words, he gently placed a kiss atop her head before the dream faded into the light of morning.

Chapter Eight

Fury

Satisfied that Snow White was finally dead, the Queen returned to the castle and continued with her rule for a long time. Still, she felt deep in her heart that she was not secure on the throne. And as the years passed by, her vanity brought her in front of the looking-glass again. Despite her witchcraft, she wondered if aging was kind to her. She stood there, gazing upon her own reflection. She was still beautiful. Anyone with wits would see that. Her subjects told her each and every day, though she suspected it was out of fear. She wondered if they truly believed her to be fair, or if there was another that had taken the place of Snow White.

"Looking-glass, Looking-glass, on the wall, who in this land is the fairest of all?"

The reflection warped in such a way that, for a moment, the Queen wanted to shatter its surface, for it made her appear ugly and old. As it steadied, the beauty of her own reflection had waned and she saw lines in her face that had not been there before.

"My dear Queen, thou art the fairest of all I see…"

In the brief time that the voice paused, relief came over the Queen. She was still beautiful. Perhaps the magicks imbued within the frame were weakening. She would resolve that soon.

"…but," the voice continued, "over the hills, in a cottage where seven men dwell, Snow White is still alive and well. And none is so fair as she."

"No! This cannot be! She is dead, for I saw it with my own eyes."

"My dear Queen, I cannot lie. This you know. Her heart still beats, still pure as snow," the voice replied.

"Quiet," she commanded. "Or I shall have your glass shattered to pieces and thrown into the moat, and your frame melted down into cups and plates."

As each day passed, her fury consumed her, and she punished those who crossed her path wrongly in the most severe fashion. The prison cells were quickly filled and public execution in varying forms occurred by the week. Queen Maurelle heard whispers that the household believed her to be mad from the overwhelming loss she had endured within a few short months. She soon quieted such rumors through a decree that whomever should speak ill of her would suffer in a way that they would wish for death. The kingdom that had once thrived and had been envied during the rule of King Owen and his lineage was now feared. Friendly trade with neighboring territories dwindled causing hardship with those who relied on such practice.

Queen Maurelle cared not for the condition of those beneath her, for her thoughts were solely on the demise of Snow White, who would now be in her thirteenth year. If the girl were to think of it, she could lay her claim to the throne, if that was her wish. Certainly, she would be a young ruler, but it was not unheard of with the proper counselors within the court. And the people had not forgotten the Princess, though they still believed her to be long gone. They would welcome her as if she had only gone on a short journey, for her beauty and kindness was the small hope they clung to during these times. And the Queen hated her even more, because she knew the truth.

"I must think of something that will truly put an end to her," she spoke aloud. Perhaps she was going mad, she thought. The child had defeated death three times. How could it be possible? As she thought on it, she wondered if the lacings had not been tight enough. Something else, then. A poison would be better to ensure the girl died. For days she researched her books until she found a spell for a poisoned comb. Surely, Snow White's hair was longer now, and she would be unable to resist something so beautiful to use as an ornament to tame her locks. Once the jeweled piece had been made, she used her craft to disguise herself once again. This time as another old woman, though different in appearance, and she began her journey to the cottage.

Chapter Nine

The Comb

Snow White had been visited each year at the cottage by the knight in black. Though he did not speak, she enjoyed his presence as it gave her some small comfort that she remembered from her childhood in the castle. She looked forward to his arrival and knew by the actions of the miners when to expect him, for she also dressed in her best clothes and took even more care to be sure that everything was in its proper place. Her ebony hair had grown longer, and she tied the red satin ribbon in place to hold it in a braid. Her red lips had grown fuller, and she grew more womanly as the years had passed. She now stood taller than the men who protected her and they built her a new bed so that she could sleep in comfort. There was nothing that she needed that they did not provide. They gave her comfort when they had heard news of her father's death and allowed her to grieve for as long as she needed. And while she still felt the emptiness of never seeing her father since that day long ago, the miners in all their efforts had become her family.

On the day that the knight arrived, he gave her the gift of the apple and once again sat in silence as she ate it. This time, Snow White had more curiosity.

"Dear sir, I mean no disrespect when I ask this of you," she said between bites. "Why do you never speak to me or show me your face? Surely, you are a kind person, for you are the only one I am allowed to see without the miners having fear in their hearts."

But the knight did not answer. Nor did he reveal his face. When she was finished with the apple, he bowed deeply and left as he always did.

In the night, as Snow White slept soundly, the young man she had dreamed of as a child lost in the forest appeared to her again.

"Sweet Snow White," he said kindly. "What a beauty you have become. Remember to always keep kindness in your heart, for beauty is nothing without it. But beware of those who would try to steal both from you. My protection has its limits, and you still have much to learn."

After his warning, they walked among the halls of a castle made of dark stone and crystal. The very same castle that she had imagined when she was younger, and she wondered again if a place so beautiful could truly exist. Her dream prince took her hand in his as he guided her from one painting to another, explaining to her the history and lineage of his land.

As the sun began to rise, he placed his hands on her shoulders and drew her in to place a kiss on her forehead before disappearing from her. Upon awaking from her dream, she could still feel the faintness of his touch. Though she had thought of him often over the years, now she wished that he was indeed real in form. He was truly handsome. More than any other she remembered from when she was young. And he was gentle and kind with her as her father had been. Most of all, he wished for her to be a fair and just ruler just as she had been told her parents were before her birth and as her father still was after the death of her mother. As Snow White performed her chores, she daydreamed of ruling by the young man's side, though she still did not know what station he held, or if he was real at all. But that mattered not to her, for her father told her that a person had true nobility if they were respectful of others.

Snow White pulled fresh baked pies from the hearth and set them on the window frame to cool before the miners returned from their work. Some distance from the cottage she heard a cry as though someone had been injured. Peering through the glass from the side, so as not to be seen, she saw an old woman seated on the ground with her hands on her ankle. Snow White wondered what to do. Of course, she had been told that she should not speak to those who passed through unless the men were with her, for the Queen might one day return if she thought Snow White still lived. But years had gone by without sign of her step-mother, and the girl had also been taught to always help those in need. She looked through the window again, and the woman was still there and appeared to be in distress. Snow White did not suspect that this old woman would do her harm, so she gathered some bandaging wraps and approached.

As Snow White neared, her feet disturbed dried leaves on the ground, appearing to startle the old woman who turned to look at her with wide eyes as her hand flew up to her heart.

"Oh! Dear child," the woman spoke with a shaking voice. "You gave me a fright. I feared that you may be a wild animal to feast on an easy meal, or a bandit who would kill me for my wares as I tend my ankle. It would seem that my unstable gait has found a rabbit den."

"You have no need to fear me," Snow White replied with a smile that shown her innocence. "I saw that you might be injured and have come with bandaging. But I must be quick, as I am not permitted to speak with strangers. However, I could not ignore a soul in need."

Deep within her black heart, the Queen recoiled seeing how beautiful Snow White had become and the kindness she was still capable of, though, outwardly she kept the illusion of her magicks.

"You are too kind, dear child," the old woman said as Snow White gently wrapped her ankle. "Please, allow me to repay you in some way."

"Oh, no," Snow White said. "I could never accept anything for what I have done. I am merely doing what I can to help you, and such things should not be done if one were to expect gifts in return. It would taint the meaning behind what is intended as an act of goodwill."

The Queen was sickened by how pure the girl was still, and wondered how she would carry out her plan to be rid of Snow White once and for all.

"I insist, sweet girl. Surely, because you do not expect repayment makes you even more deserving," she said as she reached into her basket of wares and pulled out the ornate comb. "This would look lovely in your hair."

Snow White was beguiled with the beauty of it, but still she resisted. "I really should not accept such a thing. My guardians would be displeased if they were to know."

"Are your guardians the men that are known to live in these woods?"

"Yes. They are very kind and protective of me."

"But what do they know of what a young woman desires to feel pretty? Allow me to comb your hair properly for once, while I rest a bit longer. If you like the comb, you may keep it, and I will be on my way."

The old woman caused Snow White no suspicion and let her do as she pleased. The girl recalled how it felt when the ladies of the castle would style her hair and delighted in the sensation again. Once her ebony waves had been piled upon her head, the old woman forced the comb into Snow White's locks, cutting into the skin below. Hardly a moment had passed that the poison took effect, and Snow White fell to the ground.

Wicked laughter echoed through the clearing as the evil queen cast off her illusion.

"Such a paragon of beauty, and yet so gullible and naïve. You are finished now. Nothing will save you."

As the Queen knew darkness would fall within a few short hours, she took her leave for her journey back to the castle.

When the miners returned for the evening, they came upon Snow White who appeared to be lying dead on the ground and immediately suspected that her step-mother had tricked the girl once again. They found that her hair had been styled with a comb they had not seen before and removed it, loosening her hair. Only moments had passed that Snow White came to herself, and she told the men what had happened.

"So, the Queen now preyed upon your kindness," said one of the men.

"You need to be even more vigilant in the future," said another.

"She will not stop until you are most certainly dead," spoke a third.

"Please, forgive me," Snow White said quietly, tears filling her eyes. "I only wished to help her, as I was always taught. I did not suspect her because it has been so long since my step-mother passed this way to end my life. Never did I think that she would know I still lived."

The men, though stern, comforted and consoled her, and made sure she was fed well before tucking her into her bed for a full night's rest.

Chapter Ten

The Apple

Either in confidence or arrogance, perhaps a combination, Queen Maurelle demanded a celebration in her honour upon her return to the castle. Only the most high-ranking nobles were to attend from the surrounding kingdoms and food rations for the citizens under her rule were halved in order to provide for her guests. Though this increased the suffering she had already placed upon her subjects, they feared expressing their displeasure, else they would find their heads in a basket or their necks stretched upon the gallows. The Queen's reign of terror had become so known, that even the nobles did not dare refuse her invitation and were certain to shower her with compliments on her beauty.

Nearly five years had passed and the gifts and compliments began to dwindle as the whispers among the people increased once again. Though she would never hear the source, her magicks and divining would speak to her, telling her of the wishes that King Owen was still alive or that the Princess had never gone missing. Her mood faltered and she retreated to the room which kept her prized possession. She still admired her reflection, thinking herself quite young in appearance. However, the doubts clouded her mind and darkened her heart more than ever before, as no man seemed to hold interest in her, and she still wished to have an heir to her Kingdom.

"Looking-glass, Looking-glass, on the wall, who in this land is the fairest of all?"

The reflection rippled and warped for longer than it had ever before, finally steadying to an image that was not flattering to her. More lines appeared in her face and grey hair speckled her tresses. After a long moment, the voice within answered her inquiry.

"My dear Queen, thou are the fairest of all I see…"

Good. She thought herself silly for having such thoughts. However, the voice began to speak again with some hesitation.

"…but over the hills, in a cottage where seven men dwell, Snow White is still alive and well. And none is so fair as she."

"No! She is dead! I'm certain of it," she screamed at the glass.

"My dear Queen, I cannot lie. This you know. Her heart still beats, still pure as snow. A beautiful woman is she, this much is clear. She will take the throne in her eighteenth year," the voice replied.

Queen Maurelle shook and yelled with rage, grasping the mirror and pushing it with great force to the stone floor. But the magicks in the object prevented it from shattering. She paced the floor, following the pattern that she had worn in it over the years. After a long while, she righted the looking glass with some effort.

"Snow White will die," she declared. "Even if it costs me my life. I would have this Kingdom in ruin before I allow that girl to usurp me."

"As you have no heir of your own," the looking-glass spoke, "Snow White is the true Queen of the throne."

"Never!"

Thereupon the Queen went into the depths of the castle where no one dared to venture. Knowing that she would need a more powerful poison than before, she blended several of the deadliest and imbued an apple with magick so that it would only hold poison in the half with the reddened cheek while the half with the white cheek remained pure and untouched. The spell cast upon the apple would make it impossible to resist for anyone who might gaze upon it, but should they eat it, they would surely die. Knowing that Snow White would certainly suspect if the Queen once again used the disguise of an old woman, she chose to create the illusion of a plain farmer's wife. Leaving the castle during the night, she began her journey to the clearing with the intent of finally killing Snow White before she reached her eighteenth year in less than two month's time.

Snow White cleaned the dishes after supper and studied her politics before retiring to her bed. Once asleep, she began to dream of her prince. They were in a great hall alight with candles and decorated with ornate tapestries. He taught her different styles of dance, some that she had seen when she was a child and others that were new to her. Her prince danced the steps with such a grace that at times it was difficult to match, but she learned each one and felt free from all of her worries. As if they could both sense the end of the night, they ended their revelry.

"Beautiful, Snow White," he said while gazing at her in a way that was different from her other dreams. "What troubles you so? I see sadness deep in your eyes."

"I fear that with my coming of age, my childish fancies will vanish. I am told that I will be Queen of my father's Kingdom, that I will dethrone my step-mother, for I am the rightful heir. But what joy will I have in such a thing if I do not have the prince that I dream of by my side?"

The prince laid his alabaster hand on her cheek, the coolness of it calming her and, with feather lightness, brushed his lips against her own.

"Fear not, my beloved Snow White, for I will return to you soon. Do not lose your desires only for the sake of becoming Queen. A true and good ruler will keep such things close to heart, so that they may know how to fulfill the needs of their people."

As Snow White slept, the seven miners made plans in secrecy to celebrate her coming of age and the conclusion of her studies, in which she excelled. They knew she would become a wise and generous ruler once she was able to reclaim the throne. On the day the peddlers came through the clearing on the way to the market, they chose a special gown for her to wear on that day. After a long while, the men had finally chosen a dress that nearly equaled their Princess' beauty. It was of the finest white brocade, with insets of red silk embroidered delicately with vines. The waist cinched in the front with a white satin ribbon and the sleeves flared elegantly at the wrists. To keep the chill away, as the celebration would take place when the snows began to fall, they chose a black velvet cloak. All this they had also done in secret and hid away the garments so she would not find them until the morning of celebration.

Each morning for the time that passed since the comb had poisoned her, as the men left to work in the mines, they gave Snow White the warning to not open the door to strangers, for they feared that her step-mother may still attempt to steal her life away. And each evening they returned, relieved to find that she was still safe and healthy. It would only be a few weeks before the knight in black would come to bestow a gift from the Northern Kingdom in honour of the Princess, and the miners, in their concern, requested that Snow White not venture outside unless they were near.

On a cold afternoon, while the men were away, there was a rapping at the door. Of course, Snow White did not answer, as she was abiding by the wishes of her guardians. But the visitor must have seen her pass by a window while approaching and continued to knock.

"I have come with the very last harvest of apples for the year. They are the finest yield we have had the whole season and it would be a shame to not offer such fine fruit to you as I journey to the next town," said the woman on the other side of the door.

Snow White peeked out through the window glass and saw a simple farmer's wife, but knew that she should not open the door for her. However, she did open the window to speak with her.

"I cannot let anyone in," Snow White told the woman. "I have been forbidden by my guardians.

"I shall soon get rid of my apples, for the bushel has become too cumbersome to bear. I would at least give you one before I feed the forest creatures," the woman replied.

"I dare not accept. I have been deceived before by another who feigned kindness."

"Do you fear poison? I shall share the apple with you if that is your wish," the woman said with a smile.

The fruit did look delicious, and Snow White enjoyed fresh apples. The woman sliced it in two with the dagger that hung at her waist and held the red cheeked half out to Snow White as she took a bite out of the white cheeked half. Because the apple was so cunningly made, no harm came to the woman and Snow White could no longer resist. She reached out the window and took the poisonous half, taking a bite. No sooner had she swallowed did her throat swell and close around the piece, so powerful was the poison, and she fell down dead. The wickedness of the Queen now shown on her face as she dissolved the illusion, and she laughed as she peered through the window at the Princess.

"This time those men will not be able to wake you. I have used the deadliest of all poisons. You are finally no more," she cackled. Twirling in a celebratory dance, the Queen made herself dizzy before coming to her senses and leaving the clearing to return to rule her kingdom without opposition.

Chapter Eleven

Mourning

When the miners came home in the evening, they saw that no lanterns lighted the cottage and that all was silent. Their hearts were awash with dread as they entered, and they found Snow White collapsed on the floor. They lifted her up and carried her to her bed to see whether they could find what had caused her condition. Unlacing her dress caused no change. The men placed her in a bath of water and wine, but saw no improvement, as she still did not draw breath. Combing through her damp hair did not reveal any poisons either. Their princess was dead and remained so through all their efforts. They laid her upon a bier and dressed her in the finery that was intended for her coming of age, but had now become her funeral attire. For three days the seven men wept over her, for they grieved as fathers who had lost their dearest child.

When the time came for them to bury her, they had not the heart to place her in the ground. She still appeared as if living, with a blush in her cheeks and the crimson of her lips. All agreed that they would build a coffin of glass so that her beauty, even in death, could be seen from all sides. Once they laid her inside and closed the lid, they smelted gold they had brought from the mine and wrote her name upon the glass in elegant lettering, declaring that she was King Owen's daughter, Princess of the Middle kingdom. Placing the coffin on the top of the nearby mountain, they continued to mourn, each taking turn to keep watch over her. And as the time passed, the birds mourned for her, too. First an owl, keeping vigil during the night, then a raven, which perched at her head at each sunset, and then a dove, cooing softly with each sunrise. And still, Snow White appeared unchanged and merely asleep, so beautiful did she remain beneath the glass.

When, at last, Queen Maurelle returned to the castle, she made haste to her private chamber. And though she was tired from her journey, she did not hesitate to make the inquiry of the looking-glass.

"Looking-glass, Looking-glass, on the wall, who in this land is the fairest of all?"

The mirrored surface rippled, her reflection distorting slightly before returning to its flattering image. Then a voice answered from within its depths, though it sounded somewhat saddened in its tone.

"You, my Queen. In this land thou art the fairest of all."

For a moment her breath stilled. Each time before, the looking-glass would continue on with its words. This time there was nothing but silence. The envy in her heart, mind, and spirit was finally put at ease, as much as it could be for one with such vanity. Her wicked laughter could be heard echoing throughout the halls and the courtyard as she celebrated Snow White's death.

Chapter Twelve

The Black Knight

On the evening of what should have seen the revelry of Snow White's eighteenth year, the snows fell lightly upon the mountain. The miners kept the glass clear so her beauty would not be obscured as they made toasts of ale in her honour through their tears of grief. As they kept their watch well into the evening, the knight in black appeared among them and approached the coffin, gently tracing the golden letters with his gloved hand.

In a kind tone he spoke to the men, who were surprised to hear a voice from within the helmet, as any words had been handed to them in writing. "What ill has befallen the Princess?"

"She is dead by her step-mother's hand," said one through his tears. "We did not have the heart to bury her in the ground, so beautiful is she still."

"Allow me to have the coffin and I shall see to it that you will be well rewarded."

But the men refused. "We will not part with our Princess for all the gold in the world," one of the men replied. And the others nodded firmly in agreement.

Seeing how loyal the miners were to the girl seemed to please the knight, though they could still not see his face. "Then allow me to open the coffin, for I cannot live without seeing Snow White's

beauty, and the glass is a barrier that I cannot bear."

They took pity on the knight then, for they

knew that he had shown kindness to the girl each

year of her life, and they allowed him to open the

lid. He lifted it away and gently caressed her pale

cheek with his covered fingers, then lightly touched

her blood red lips. Suddenly, he stilled and

remained motionless for several long moments. The

miners watched without a word spoken between

them. Then the knight slowly removed his gauntlets

and bascinet, placing them on the ground. He lifted

Snow White up into his arms as if in an embrace,

his back facing the miners so they could not observe

his actions or his visage. He placed his lips upon the

most tender part of her throat and drained the

poison out with her blood. Laying her back down

with the utmost care, he removed a flask from his belt and parted her lips that he could pour the contents into her. Within a moment, Snow White opened her eyes and coughed, expelling the last bit of poisoned apple that the elixir had not dissolved. She sat up and, once more, appeared full of life.

"Oh," she cried. "What has happened?"

"All is well, for you are with me now," replied the knight. "You were but a whisper away from death, so powerful was the poison within you. But I have given you the gift of eternity. I love you more than anything in this world, Snow White. Please come with me to my father's palace and take place at my side as my wife."

With his words, the miners came to understand who the mysterious knight was and, immediately bending the knee, bowed their heads low. Snow White, who could see him clearly by the light of the torches nearby, knew him for the man she had only ever seen in her dreams.

"My Prince! You have truly come for me. I feared that you were but a figment of my mind."

The knight lifted her from the glass coffin, carefully setting her feet on the ground and holding her in a gentle embrace.

"You may call me William, my love," he said. "I have watched over you, even before your birth, just as I promised your mother, Queen Fiona, ensuring you would not fall to the curse that afflicted her. When your step-mother would have had you killed by her huntsman, I sent a bear cub to take your place for the slaughter. Each apple that I bestowed upon you from year to year was imbued with the same blood elixir that saved you as an infant. The blood of the people of the Northern kingdom is such that our lives are extended well beyond that of others. It is also what has prevented you from succumbing fully to each murderous attempt by your wicked step-mother. But for you to grow into such a beautiful woman, I could only give you small amounts, for anymore would have done what could not be undone. Now, your life has been spared and poisons will no longer affect your constitution. This is my gift to you and agreed upon by all of the Northern peoples, because you are the beloved daughter of King Owen, and it is but a small repayment for all he had done for us."

Indeed, Snow White felt differently than she had before, and she knew that her life was now changed. But she would now be with her prince as she had been in her dreams, and she was happy. William placed a finger under her chin and gently laid a kiss upon her blood red lips.

"Your mother also wished that you would find a love not unlike what she and your father shared. Only if you are willing would I ask for marriage."

"You are my beloved prince," Snow White replied. "I would have no other by my side."

William kissed her once again, then turned to the miners who were still on bended knee.

"You may rise," he told them. "You have all done well in caring for Snow White and teaching her the things that her mother wished so that she would become a kind and just ruler of the Middle

Kingdom. And now, she will further seal the unity of the Middle and North by willingly becoming my bride, and together we will restore her kingdom to what it once was. Behold your rightful Queen."

Chapter 13

The Wedding

The union of Snow White and Prince William was arranged with such splendour, with a grand wedding and even grander feast to follow. All of the households of the Middle and North kingdoms were summoned to attend. The character of the Prince's bride was held to the utmost secrecy as to entice those of the Middle kingdom who would sate their curiosity. All that was known was that she was not of the North. Queen Maurelle was also bidden to the feast, and she arrayed herself in her most elegant gown and adornments. Many wicked thoughts were in her mind as she stood

before her looking-glass to admire her beauty.
Perhaps she would entrance the Prince to steal him
away from his bride, becoming Queen of another
kingdom, so greedy was she for power. Or she
might seduce the King of that land, bear him an heir,
and put an end to the young Prince's life.

"Looking-glass, Looking-glass, on the wall.
Who in this land is the fairest of all?"

The image rippled and shifted and became
more warped than she had ever seen, before settling
once again on her reflection.

"Dear, Queen. Of all in this Kingdom thou
art the fairest I see. But the young Queen in the
North is fairer by far than thee."

She raged at the answer and did not think to
ask anymore. Uttering the most vile curses she

paced the room not knowing what to do. She thought to be absent from the wedding, but her mind would not be at peace. Not seeing the young Queen for herself would surely drive her mad. And so she called forth her finest carriage and made a fast journey to the North.

Though Queen Maurelle had not been in attendance for the wedding, she entered the great hall where the feast was already well underway. Servants milled about filling cups and dishes as they were emptied by the many guests. She recognized some as noble families of the Middle Kingdom. Elaborate tapestries lined the dark stone walls and plush cushions seated every person at the long tables. Torches and candles aplenty lit the room that would otherwise be cast in darkness, as there were no windows to be seen. Musicians were in the corner playing merry tunes. The serving table was lined with only the finest of foods. Boars' heads and stuffed pheasants, pork pies and roasted mallards. The heady scents of mulled wine and cooking spices filled the air. As the centerpiece stood a spun sugar sculpture of two swans, the gentle curves of their necks forming a heart shape. As she walked further into the hall, expecting that she would be seated near the royal family, given her own station, the din of the guests seemed to quiet. In her wicked mind, Queen Maurelle thought how they must know to give her their attention, despite the reason for the festivities. When she had finally come to the center of the room, she was frozen still with rage and fear, for she recognized Snow White seated next to the Prince, both dressed in the finest of wedding clothes.

"What is this trickery," she cried into the now silent hall.

With but a small gesture from Snow White, iron slippers were pulled from the fire by one of the servants with a pair of tongs and placed before Queen Maurelle. Though she thought to escape, she was held firmly in place by two guards who appeared next to her as if by a magic she had not known.

"Surely you would not be this cruel to your dear step-mother, Snow White," she pleaded.

Prince William stood and, with a stern countenance, spoke to her.

"You shall address my bride as 'Your majesty', as she is the true and rightful Queen of the Middle Kingdom."

Snow White gently placed her hand on top of his and rose to her feet. As if by a mere glance at the guards, they began to force Queen Maurelle's feet into the red-hot slippers.

"But King Owen taught you to be just and kind," she screamed. "Where is your mercy?"

"Dance for our guests," Snow White responded. "Plead for their mercy, not mine."

The two guards forced Queen Maurelle into a danse macabre, her feet blistering painfully and her body willing to give out at any moment. After what seemed an eternity, the guards ceased in their action and held her in place once again. Snow White then approached with the same grace that the people of the North were rumoured to possess. Indeed, she seemed to hold their ethereal beauty as well, making her even more fair than the evil queen remembered.

"I am indeed as just and kind as my mother wished, as my father taught, and as my guardians nurtured with their lessons," she spoke in a calm demeanor as she stood before Queen Maurelle. "I am just in that I decreed a suitable punishment for the cruelty and malice you imposed upon the citizens of my Kingdom. I am merciful in that I will ensure you will die quickly, though you sought to murder me five times over. I am kind in that I will restore my father's kingdom to what it once was, wherein the people will no longer live in fear of those who should lead them with compassion and grace, or live in squalor while those of high station live in excess at the cost of their subjects. I have become exactly as my parents wished and what you made me to be. I am the rightful Queen of my father's lands and have sealed the union with the North Kingdom on this day. Your illegitimate claim to the throne and reign of terror has come to an end."

The former queen's eyes grew wide with this new knowledge, despite the agonizing pain that wracked her body and charred feet. Snow White moved closer to Maurelle and sank her teeth deeply into her step-mother's throat, consuming her bitter blood until the woman dropped down dead.

THE END